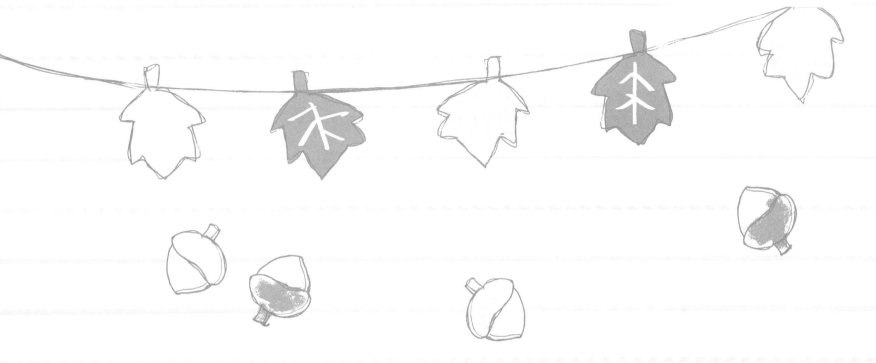

HELLO
SCHOOL!

words and pictures by

Priscilla Burris

NANCY PAULSEN BOOKS

*In honor of Miss Molly, who loved all the preschoolers she taught,
and for my beloved Riggin Avenue (now Hamasaki) Elementary School*

Nancy Paulsen Books
an imprint of Penguin Random House LLC
375 Hudson Street
New York, NY 10014

Library of Congress Cataloging-in-Publication Data
Names: Burris, Priscilla, author.
Title: Hello school! / Priscilla Burris.
Description: New York, NY : Nancy Paulsen Books, [2018]
Summary: "Children have fun at school experiencing familiar classroom activities for the first time"
—Provided by publisher.
Identifiers: LCCN 2017038159 | ISBN 9780399172021 (hardcover : alk. paper)
| ISBN 9780698175693 (ebook) | ISBN 9780698175686 (ebook) |
Subjects: | CYAC: First day of school—Fiction. | Schools—Fiction.
Classification: LCC PZ7.B94065 Hel 2018 | DDC [E]—dc23
LC record available at https://lccn.loc.gov/2017038159
Manufactured in China by RR Donnelley Asia Printing Solutions Ltd.
ISBN 9780399172021
1 3 5 7 9 10 8 6 4 2

Design by Eileen Savage. Text set in Farao Book and Nouveau Crayon.
The illustrations were created with ink pens, pencils, paper, and digital brushes.

School starts!

We are welcomed.

Everything is new!

Our teacher is
new to us . . .

and we are new
to her!

A place for everything.

For our stuff. And for us!

It's circle time.

We sing our good morning song.

We learn when we listen . . .

And we don't interrupt.

Snack time.

We say thank you!
We are good helpers.

Oops!

My Mom says that's the way the cookie crumbles!

Fall is here!

It gets cold outside.
We stay warm inside.

Nature rocks!

We look, we listen, we explore!

Counting is fun!

Hooray for recess!

We swing. We slide. We soar.

Quiet time.

We read. We rest.
We nest!

Mrs. Friend,
Kevin is hibernating
TOO LOUD!

Learning our letters.

Letters make words.

We make rhymes:

We are all artists

in our own way!

We say our good-byes!

To our teacher.
To our friends.

It was the
best day ever!

Want to play on
my new swing set?

And to our school.